Sinkholes are every-
where now.

Welcome to Christoph Keller's *America the Beautiful & Other Indictments*, whose title is as misleading as its aperçus are biting original. Like pinpricks penetrating a dark veil, these glittering insights are arranged as cunningly as they are crafted, for a constellation greater than the sum of its shards.

– Madison Smartt Bell, author, *All Souls Rising*, *Master of the Crossroads*, and *Zero db*

Some observations from the European press on Christoph Keller's latest novel in German, *Der Boden unter den Füssen (The Ground Beneath the Feet)*:

A poetic and optimistic book.
– *WDR5 (Westdeutscher Rundfunk)*

Magical!
– *Style*

A narrative jewel.
– *Neue Zürcher Zeitung am Sonntag*

Who travels, they say, educates themselves. But maybe they only pollute the world.
– *Südkurier*

… featherlight, sparklingly elegant as Duke Ellington's piano.
– *kulturzeitschrift (Austria)*

America the Beautiful & other Indictments

A Meaningful Life 2.0

Christoph Keller

Text-Only Edition

Reprobate / GobQ Books
Portland, Oregon
2020

for Peter Weber

Reprobate / GobQ Books

America the Beautiful
& other Indictments
A Meaningful Life 2.0
Text-Only Edition
Christoph Keller

Reprobate / GobQ Books

ISBN 978-1-64764-361-4, Apr. 2020 ||| $12.00

© Christoph Keller, 2020

All rights reserved. No part of this book may be reproduced in any form without written permission of the copyright owners.

The images in this book have been reproduced with knowledge & prior consent of the artists concerned, & no responsibility is accepted by the producer, publisher, or printer for any infringement of copyright or otherwise, arising from the contents of this publication. Every effort has been made to ensure that credits accurately comply with information supplied. We apologize for any inaccuracies that may have occurred & will resolve inaccurate or missing information in any subsequent reprinting of the book.

10 9 8 7 6 5 4 3 2

||| Cover & Interior Design: rvb ||| T. Warburton y Bajo ||| cover & int. estampia, courtesy var. postal services ||| enso: rvb |||

Acknowledgments:

Quadrant (Sydney, 9/2014): Guest, Afterlife, Conclusion, Solo Flight, My New Neighbors, My Son, Sabbatical. *Lampish Press* (Greensboro, 2015): Guest, Pearl Street, Afterlife, Conclusion, Solo Flight, Story, Habitat, Windows, My New Neighbors, New Mayor, Family Eyes, Birthday, Friendship, My Son, Voice Mail, Sabbatical, A Meaningful Life, Freehold, Blind Date. *Saiten* (St. Gallen, 11/2015): Blood Count, New Rhumba, Sound Seekers. *Quadrant* (Sydney, 11/2016): Habitat, Windows, New Mayor, Birthday, Voice Mail, Blind Date. *Birutjatio Press* (Santiniketan, 2016): Guest, Pearl Street, Explorer, Afterlife, Conclusion, Story, Habitat, My New Neighbors, New Mayor, Family Eyes, Birthday, Friendship, My Son, Voice Mail, Sabbatical, My Friend Mindy, A Meaningful Life, Freehold, Blind Date. *Five2One Magazine* (online, 4/2017): Creation Myth, Hellos, Our Country, Metamorphosis. *Sand Journal* (Berlin, 6/2017): Knowledge (nominated for a Pushcart Prize), Zosimo's Dream. *Quadrant* (Sydney, 3/2017): Story, Family Eyes, Friendship, A Meaningful Life, Freehold. *8 Wespress* (online, 2017): My New Neighbors. *Gobshite Quarterly; Little Beirut, Oregon* (6/2018): Solo Flight, My Friend Mindy, Blood Count, New Rhumba, Sound Seeker (translated into German, Croatian, Lithuanian, Bangla, Russian & Spanish—available as separate chapbook: *Appendix A: Soundseekers*). *Best Small Fictions, selected by Aimee Bender*, Braddock Avenue Books, (fall 2018): Solo Flight. *Saiten 5/2018 unter dem Titel Romantiquane Signersignale*, Roman Signer zum 80. Geburtstag) Der Fallensteller; Der Zeitstörer; Der Naturärgerer; Der Ensömeister; Der Dingbeleber; Der Physikpraktizierer; Der Elementarschauer; Der Bildhauer.

MOGADIS

I. Meaningful Lives — 13

- Brief History of Art — 14
- Knowledge — 15
- Knowledge — 16
- Explorer — 17
- Guest — 18
- Windows — 19
- Likes — 20
- Habitat — 21
- Continuity — 22
- Metamorphosis — 23
- In a Daze — 24
- Infallibly — 25
- Sabbatical — 26
- Hellos — 27
- Photograph — 28
- Hubris — 29
- Likes — 30
- Soledad — 31
- Afterlife — 32
- Conclusion — 33

◊ ◊ ◊

- Solo Flight — 35
- Blood Count — 36
- My Friend Mindy — 37
- New Rhumba — 38
- Sound Seekers — 39

◊ ◊ ◊

- These Boots — 41
- Zosimos' Dream — 42
- Memories — 43
- Vocation — 44
- Europe During the Rain — 45
- Time and The River — 46

II. The Practitioner of Physics * — 51

- The Trapper — 52
- The Time-Teaser — 54
- The Nature-Annoyer — 55
- The Ensō-Master — 56
- The Thing-Invigorator — 58
- The Practitioner of Physics — 59
- The Elementary Watcher — 60
- The Insight-Generator — 61

III. America the Beautiful — 63

- New Mayor — 64
- Freehold — 65
- Friendship — 66
- A Meaningful Life — 67
- My Son — 68
- Likes — 69
- Our Country — 70
- Winner — 71

America the Beautiful	72
Winner	73
New Address	74
The 18th Constitutional Crisis	75
The Life Maximizers	76
My New Neighbors	77
Family Eyes	78
Birthday	79
Patterns	80
Pleshcheev	81
Likes	82
Bronx Zoo	83
Equilibrium	84
Again	85
Crawl	86
Winner	87
Main Street	88
Creation Myth	89
Brief History of Mankind	90

*) *The Practitioner of Physics, tr. fr. the German, Douglas Spangle w/ Christoph Keller*

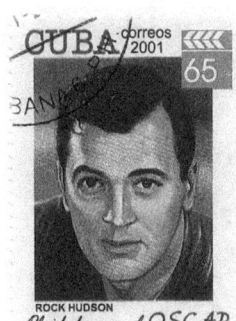

I.

Meaningful Lives

Brief History of Art

The greatest sculptor is nature, the sculptor said, then planted a tree.

Knowledge

Trishna believes everything anyone says about God. It worries me that she might have heard of the early gnostic Basilides who said what defines God is that he is not.

Knowledge

The Koyukon of Alaska believe the caribou song arrives when she's ready. The hunter wakes up with her song in his mouth and knows where to find her.

Explorer

Don't we all want to be the kind of cursor that clicks through to the other side of the screen, the arrow that flies out of the document?

Guest

So sorry I'm not home, but I just can't deal with you. You have the keys to my apartment and mailbox. In a few days you'll get another note. Water the plants, but not the bonsai on my desk. It's hard to water a bonsai.

Windows

Here I am again. Hiding again. For how long? Expecting what? The five porthole windows in the concrete walls are five faces without lips or a nose or even eyes, glaring at me. Five rays of light blossom through the darkness, a five-fingered flower where I live.

Likes

Jim loves Bruno, his and Jane's puppy, a mix between a dachshund and a Saint Bernard, but he hates his work as a dispatcher for a provider of after-hours facility management services. He experiences both feelings with an intensity new to him. I love you, he says. I'm asking you what you *like*, Jane shoots back. I like your new haircut, Jim finally says. I can't say I love it, but I also don't hate it.

Habitat

We live underground. We go as deep into the earth as we can. Depending on the territory, we use the groundhog or the subway tunnels. Underneath the old cities, there are still wooden pipes which make some of us nostalgic, others nervous. Moving through roots is hard—they're sticky; caves make us merry and frisky: they're our playgrounds. Living in the sewer system can feel demeaning but, eventually, it pays off. I've met up with many an affable rat and even the occasional cockroach. Some I now consider friends.

Continuity

The death Gogol didn't die. The unfinished story Kafka didn't write about the death Gogol didn't die. The movie project based on the unfinished story Kafka didn't write about the death Gogol didn't die that Fellini never realized. The original music for Fellini's unrealized movie project based on the unfinished story Kafka didn't write about the death Gogol didn't die that Bowie heard in his head but didn't write down. The novel of the untold story of that masterpiece taking shape in my mind.

Metamorphosis

He woke up from uneasy dreams. Slowly inhaling, strongly exhaling, he began to feel calmer. Soon he stopped worrying about packing up the cloth samples or whether he'd be late for his 8 a.m. customer. Time was both over and eternal. Nothing became no thing. Gregor Samsa was fully awake.

In a Daze

There's only one way to achieve perfection in a work of art, and that's by not making that work of art, Orrin likes to say. Easy for him: *his* sculptures are in every major museum in the world. Leaving Orrin's studio in a daze, Barry's struggling to find his way home. His first work of art, refusing to emerge from his mind, is clearly destined for perfection.

Infallibly

I AM AN AMATEUR AND I INTEND TO STAY THAT WAY FOR THE REST OF MY LIFE. -- ANDRE KERTESZ, is stenciled in Didot typeface on the wall in our living room. Infallibly, whenever there's a silence in the conversation, someone will look at me, then at the quote above my head and say, I disagree. Infallibly I will respond, shouldn't we all love what we do?, hoping for more silence.

Sabbatical

I support my wife in everything, even in her arguments against me. It's this highly developed empathy of mine that makes it hard to live with me. Nuala is a distinguished professor at City College; her field is interpersonal neurobiology. She's now on a sabbatical from me, traveling to the last places on earth without internet access, including Samoa, Tristan da Cunha, most of the Grand Canyon and some of the Black Forest. Nuala made it clear that she expects to come back to a different me.

Hellos

A wolf appears. Or is it a bull? It could be a bear. She took the picture on a tour of the Chauvet Cave, behind the guide's back. Photography is strictly forbidden in the cave: it is home to the oldest known examples of man-, or rather, woman-made, paintings, going back 30,000 years. Maybe more. Art older than art itself; hellos from the world in which we all once lived.

for a m m

Photography

She seems taller when the sun touches her, which it does now, through our eighth-floor living room window. It's only natural that she chose the art of light as her profession.

Hubris

In my novels, Reed says, I gave you all the qualities you will never have. I worked so hard at our relationship. Five novels in eight years. Who you are now that I'm leaving is not my problem anymore.

Likes

Tomeika loves Mary, her and Linnéa's three-and-a-half year-old daughter, their second, but she hates her work as a Scattered-site Public Housing Manager for the Borough of Queens. She experiences both feelings with an intensity new to her. I love your new haircut, he says. I asked you what is it you *like*, Linnéa shoots back. I like Cardi B, Tomeika finally says. I can't say I love her, but I also don't hate her.

Soledad

Soledad has a tendency to talk a lot, and at length, especially about Soledad. Soledad did this, Soledad says, and Soledad did that. Soledad says things like, The only water Soledad carries is her own, and Soledad fucking Soledad is not your bitch, and it's not about, and has never been, Soledad's hair, and Soledad is not a troll. The more Soledad talks, the less Soledad likes to be interrupted. And this is that, and that is it.

Afterlife

What happens after you die, Joseph believes, is you keep doing over and over what you were doing the exact moment you died. These days he's spending as much time as he can doing what he likes best: sliding sideways in the mud in his pick-up truck, looking into his son's brown eyes, drinking cold beer; and as little as he can of what he likes the least: seeing his older sister, taking out the trash, walking into spider webs.

Conclusion

Ray's dreams tell him what to do: to throw a lit match into a mailbox; make a donation; push someone off a roof; play the lottery. The dreams come with all the necessary information: Jim's mailbox, 3F; $27, to the Police Benevolent Association; Greg, off the ConEd Building; 8, 9, 19, 34, 39, 43. Whatever his dreams tell him to do, Ray does. Nothing ever goes wrong. I've weighed the pros and cons of Ray's dreams. I've explored the moral and ethical ramifications. Some of the things Ray does don't seem quite right. But I've come to the conclusion that certainty in life is worth the compromise.

◊ ◊ ◊

Solo Flight

Although it wasn't a number he recognized, Adan, a fruit street vendor in the Meatpacking District, his earpieces at the ready, accepted the call. Somebody playing music. Adan could tell it was one of Coltrane's late long solos. Once Rashied Ali, who played in Coltrane's last recorded concert, bought fruit from Adan—a mango and a handful of peaches. Rashied said that Trane had flown to God on the waves of his last solo. An odd-looking fellow in orange sneakers and a yellow umbrella under his arm stood at his stand. Adan hadn't seen him approach. The man examined the fruit for a long time, squeezing a melon with his fingertips, weighing an apple in his open palm. Finally, he bought two pears for $1.25 each, and the music in Adan's head stopped.

Blood Count

I can't be you anymore. I hardly have the strength to be me, Shelby told Horton. It was what Strayhorn had said to Ellington, when Strayhorn was dying of esophageal cancer. When Horton left—he had started going to church, just like Ellington had started writing sacred music at the end of Strayhorn's life—Shelby played *Blood Count* on his phone. It was Strayhorn's final composition, written just before he died in this very ward at East Harlem's Hospital for Joint Diseases. Pulling up his gown, popping open his abdominal tap and pouring the cognac in it, Shelby felt the moan of the music enter.

for e&m

My Friend Mindy

Fear of death was why Ellington delayed everything, even titling his finished songs. Mindy is homebound due to an unidentified virus she thinks she picked up on her recent trip to Quito. She now stops in the middle of writing a text; pauses a Netflix show before it's over; heats up her broth but never lets it boil; looks away while a bird or a plane is flying past her window; cuts short her dreams and wills herself out of sleep a few moments before she would have woken up anyway. I suspect she's on the verge of figuring out how not to finish her virus infection. Never one to put anything off, I fear I've started all this too late, Mindy tells me during my visit and begs me not to leave but I'm already halfway out the door.

New Rhumba

She had reserved this table at the left of the stage so she could see Jamal at the keyboard. He started his set with "New Rhumba," her favorite. Spreading his fingers, he let the universe come through; creating spaces, he left the music behind, like a beautiful memory. She had booked this table for all ten sets but she was already gone.

Sound Seekers

I can't do this from a physical level anymore, Master Higgins said, letting his gaze linger on the instruments in the living room. Acoustic guitar, Indian drums, African percussion, trap set; Akhi's saxophones, piano, Tibetan oboe, tarogato, flutes, more clarinets. I won't be there, Master Higgins said, but I will always be with you. After a while, he smiled and played dut-dut-dut to Akhi's Spanish tune, swinging, dancing, raising the music.

◊ ◊ ◊

These Boots

The longer you look at an object, the more alive it becomes, John said. We could barely keep up with his pace. When he finally stopped in front of MooShoes on Orchard—known for footwear that was both made cruelty-free *and* no crime against fashion—we grouped behind him. Those, he said and pointed at a gorgeous pair of black velvet ankle boots with a 9-cm silver heel. I was itching to send Iris a picture—they had "Iris" written all over them—but pulling out your phone was a big no-no in John's world. So we watched John looking at the boots. He looked and looked and looked, and we watched and watched and watched. These boots are not going to walk away by themselves, someone said. Go home, Dhonielle, John barked over his shoulder. This is not what this exercise is about. This is about looking. And home Dhonielle went while the rest of us are still here, watching watching watching John looking.

Zosimos' Dream

I start telling my neighbor Frank about my dream last night, but he cuts me short. I don't dream, he says, and I don't want to hear what other people dream, especially people who live in one of my buildings. I tell him anyway. The priest Ion mistakenly turns me into spirit and, as a consequence, he becomes something neither spirit nor matter. Frank looks shaken. Seventeen people, including him, live in this building. Frank owns another three in Massapequa on Long Island, two in Chappaqua in northern Westchester County, and one more here in the Turtle Bay neighborhood of Manahatta.

Memories

Place: Room 312 of the Heldrich Hotel & Conference Center. Time: 0243 p.m. of April 11, 2001. Sue was about to head off to Rutgers University to moderate a panel on *The Interpretation of Dreams*. That was where and when the itching started. Now she regards Room 312 as a portal from one Sue to another. She has gone back several times—same time, same room—to see whether the itching would subside. It got worse. By now, Sue's skin is a crusty red except for a few white lines, furrows that made her think of the farm in Minnesota where she grew up. That was the first Pre-itching-Sue memory. She kept scratching until thin streams of blood trickled along the furrows of her Minnesota skin. I know you're in there, Non-itching Sue! The faint voice she hears encourages her to keep scratching.

Vocation

Whatever job Andrey applies for, he gets. These include plumber mechanic at NYU Langone, commercial & airline planning intern at Jet-Blue Airways in Hoboken, NJ; DMV customer service representative & road tester in Juneau, AK; robotics automation technical architect in Costa Mesa, CA. When Andrey is accepted for a job, he immediately reports to the company that he's no longer available. From time to time he gets in touch with one of the "Andreys" as he calls those who did get "his" job. He wants to know how they like their jobs. They all love them. I'm an "Andrey"—the runner-up for the position of career coach in Bethlehem, PA. Andrey and I are friends now. This gives me access to his unique knowledge about jobs and how to get them. Here's my card.

Europe During the Rain

You do know your papers are not in order, don't you? the customs officer said. The painter nodded. He had spent a year in five different internment camps, and now he hoped to escape to America. It was May 1, 1941. His paintings were lined up along the walls of a small French-Spanish border train station. Naked women, their skin overgrown with grass and moss, stems and branches growing heads with sharp-toothed mouths and sad eyes, birds marching determinedly on human legs. If your papers were in order, you could take the train to Spain, the customs officer said. My duty, however, is to make you board the other train, the one that'll take you back. You do have talent though, he added, watching more and more people gather, losing themselves in the paintings. Go now. Go—and choose the right train.

Time and The River

My piss is flowing like time. There's a small raft on the river, and on the raft, there's a black alarm clock. The alarm starts ringing, but I can't tell the time. It's early, it's late. My piss has stopped flowing. The clock is so far downriver that I can't tell whether it's still ringing. I've never felt so far away from home.

Lou's headache is only in his head.

Honey, I love you too, but there's just so much to do.

I know what the attention of a fruit fly is.

Where can I find out less?

ii.
The Practitioner of Physics

Tr. fr. the German, Douglas Spangle with Christoph Keller

The Trapper

This time, he's falling in the trap, not nature. Is it a trap when one sets the trap oneself? Maybe he's asking himself this now in the film we watch as he begins to walk again. We only see him from behind, so we assume that his gaze is fixed on the distance, not on the ice under his feet. It's not about whether he reaches the other bank. This is a meditation on walking, but also more than that: an increasingly existential drama. Anxiety seizes us. Proceed carefully, we want to call to him. Not so brashly. But isn't he walking more securely with each step? As the ice finally collapses under his feet, walking becomes falling. Now it is the camera that has become unsteady: it wobbles. Whoever is filming may feel the urge to help him, but that's not their job. We watch as he struggles to pull himself to safety. How does one proceed with proper caution when one breaks through ice? He's too far away from shore for the ice-breaking method. Struggling on the ice, whacking away, he'd be digging his grave of ice. Is a lifesaving team around? We know he survived. He knows that even though he escaped from nature this time, in the end he cannot. Knowing this makes him face that moment calmly. We calm down ourselves.

The Time-Teaser

That time has a particular structure is a popular superstition. He has other notions. Time is in flux, nothing he can do about it, nor does he want to. What he can do is tease time a little. Frequently he blasts holes into the tick-tock of time. Now he's planning something different. He flies far away, to Poland, and travels to a river he knows well. He brings some wood and a clock. He builds a small raft and mounts the clock on it. He sets the alarm and allows time to flow over the river. With a couple of black-and-white photographs he's outwitting the colors of nature. The clock reads 11:09. He's looking at the clock on the raft until it disappears. He doesn't know where it will be when it rings. He has made a where from a when.

The Nature-Annoyer

Nature doesn't really annoy him—on the contrary, he loves her: she forms the backdrop of many of his experiments. This time, however, it's all about annoying nature. Just a little. She won't take offense, even if her humor is not conciliatory. All he needs is a red ball. And water. Dynamic, so flowing water. Water that is strong enough to make a fist. No need to go to Poland for that. He needs a mountain stream, and there are plenty of those here. He's already in one, wading around in his fishing boots. Nature grins: it takes her a split second, and the jester is sopping. He squeezes the ball into the drainpipe so that the water can't drain anymore. It hisses and rages. It really sounds like anger even if nobody knows for sure what anger sounds like. Finally the water makes its fist and punches the ball. The stream bursts out. Nature laughs. See! He laughs too. He has taught nature to laugh at herself. The water is everywhere, even sloshing into his boots. It would not be the first time he caught a cold at work.

The Ensō-Master

Learn what is proper, as was often said to him. And if you want to be an artist for sure, at least be a painter. Those Pollock drips that rake in millions even impress the philistines. And yet again he has an idea. Often you have ideas to get rid of ideas. Here it is. An easel stands in a meadow before a forest. On it is a white canvas, at it a stool. At some distance, on the ground a small box. With the sure stride of someone who has walked over ice until it broke he enters the video and sits down energetically. He dips the brush he brought into the can he also brought. Then he leans a bit forward on his stool, holding the brush in his right hand close to the canvas, and waits. We all wait. Half of life is waiting. Smoke begins to rise from the box. Although we suspect a bit what will happen, like the painter he is in this moment, we're spooked too. When the box explodes: he jerks, and a black smudge appears on the canvas. What we see looks like a point, and that's also what the work is called: *Point*. But when the camera moves closer, we see that it's not really a point. What we see seems Japanese. It could be the beginning of an

Ensō. In any case, it's the clenched expression of a moment that an Ensō master practices a lifetime to get right in one stroke. His painting also looks right. He too has practiced for this moment his whole life.

The Thing-Invigorator

Things are dead, any child knows that. Wrong! Any child knows that things are alive. Things are only dead when the child is grown. Then the thing is just a chair. Or a table. Or a pair of fishing boots. And yet, all you have to do is put on the boots and they carry you. Even though seven-league boots are not his cup of tea. Tea has nothing to do with boots. But what if water gets into your boots? Aren't those specially made to keep water out? Eureka! He applies a charge of explosives to the inside of his fishing boots, fills them with water and ignites them. Boom! Boots become geysers, high fountains of water gush out of them. Glorious! Water sculptures, with a very brief lifespan. Geysers, what a fine word, captured in a photograph. Perhaps his most beautiful picture. It's even more beautiful how the dancing boots live on in memory. Things are alive.

The Practitioner of Physics

It is not that all of a sudden apples fall up to trees, and yet we think this is possible when the seven windows of the abandoned hotel open and seven chairs fly out. At first it really looks as though chairs could fly. Where would a flock of chairs fly? South? Anywhere but south? We're not dealing with an upside-down world here, but still the one in which apples fall from trees. But it is also one in which chairs fly out of windows. Which finally do crash, loud and hard, on the asphalt parking lot in front of the hotel, splintering and reordering themselves in very unchairwise ways. Some of the chairs are still chairs, even if they can't be sat upon anymore; others were chairs only in a previous life: now they are fallen birds. Unfortunately birds do fall from the sky, even if, in that case, they're more likely to smash like apples than to break into pieces like chairs. Therewith, experiment ended. I haven't studied physics, I practice it, he says. The universe could say that about itself too.

The Elementary Watcher

Are we building virtual realities, because we no longer wish to live in ours? Do we yearn for other worlds because we still have not grasped ours? Does it urge us to a beyond because we simply mismanaged this side? Question upon question, each one scarier than the next. So better not ask ourselves any of these. We fear ourselves in this world for we understand that it is we who damage it more and more. And still change nothing. Simply go on. Will go well. Lifting off, little remote-controlled helicopters, whirring hectically around our room, splat!, one of us smacks against the wall, one into the ceiling, a third into another. We're already lying with broken rotors on the floor. Twitching away a bit mechanically, silently wrecked. A brief pleasure. Madly comic. Above all, mad.

The Insight-Generator

And so there he stands on the edge of a geyser, in Iceland, naturally. He wears a windbreaker with a hood, safety goggles, heavy shoes. A geyser is a spring of water, built by no one, that throws hot water up periodically. The water bursts into a sculpture, dissolves instantly and slaps back to earth. Also on him and the umbrella he has hastily opened to protect himself. It's still not as he imagined. He steps three paces nearer the geyser. Waits. He could tease the geyser with soapy water, so it would rain faster. But that would injure the geyser. And anyway, waiting is part of it. Again the water gushes high, again he opens his umbrella, but his feet are now in the boiling-hot water. He runs away fast. The feet are scalded, but the work is done. It can't fail as success is not a condition of his work. It is a precise experiment designed to set chance free. What happens, happens, and now it has happened. His gain is an insight; what we see is an image. How much of this insight we want to intuit is up to us. But he has given us something to work with.

III.

America the Beautiful

New Mayor

Except on New Year's, Memorial Day, Fourth of July, Labor Day, Thanksgiving and Christmas, when the impounds are closed, the new mayor's efforts to tow illegally parked FBI cars has led to longer lines at the precincts and a spike in privacy.

Freehold

Growing up in Freehold, Alice spent her summer afternoons in the backyard, waiting for the cicadas to hatch. Oozing their way out of their eggs, they dropped from their pencil-thin twigs and speedily burrowed into the earth. They sucked tree roots and breathed soil, living their lives of clarity. I'm only twenty-two, Alice tells herself. It's not too late to go back to Freehold.

Friendship

My oldest friend Zakary has moved to Nova Zombia. I've warned him. He knows how dangerous it is to be exposed to the living. The drought is global, we're all hungry. I'm trying not to think of the last time I spotted a human. Someone else got to it first. Few travel nowadays. Those who still do all bring back messages from Zakary.

A Meaningful Life

The moment Lorraine saw the postcard-size ad in her mailbox, she knew she'd undergo the procedure. NO MORE IMPULSIVE ACTIVITIES! NO MORE NON-STOP FUN! NO MORE COMPULSIVE TRAVELING! Now that her back is expertly broken just below her neck, the urge to do anything without giving it some thought first is slowly ebbing away.

My Son

When my son came back he wasn't my son anymore. I gather he's the one shooting people from the roof of that derelict building downtown. I was always suspicious of that building.

Likes

Adahy loves Lana, his and Sanchali's neighbor, a dedicated gardener, but he hates his work as Health, Safety and Environmental Officer for Glencore Coal South Africa. He experiences both feelings with an intensity new to him. I love Cardi B, he says. I am asking you what is it you *like*, Sanchali shoots back. I like sex, Adahy finally says. I can't say I love it, but I also don't hate it.

Our Country

Leave, I implore my sister. The more passionately I talk, the more probingly she looks at me. They've rationed our food, they're poisoning our air and making our roads impassable. They stoned our neighbor's daughter because her father mispronounced the name of the new god. I talk and talk. My sister never blinks, never looks away. Eyes and mouth lock. My mouth, her eyes.

Winner

I've never been faithful, and I've never told the truth. Whoever crossed my path, I've deceived, whoever touched me, I've infected. I've murdered many, some just because I could. I'm turning lakes into deserts, I'm staring at the sun until it goes blind.

America the Beautiful

Deny, deny, deny. That's how I live with it. High school shooting? Never happened. Survivors? Crisis actors. How do I live with myself? I'm a crisis actor. I never happened.

Winner

Now that so many leaders are thugs it's a good thing our leader is also a thug, the powerful op-ed columnist writes. Thugs understand the thug mind. Thugs sense weakness and hit hard. Thugs know how to bully thugs. Thugs gotta thug. Thugs speak thug. Don't take this as an endorsement of our leader.

New Address

Say you always wanted to live in New York but can't afford it, Cooper said. That's easy now that we've expanded the grid of Manhattan. Without moving, you now live on East $14{,}472^{nd}$ Avenue at $70{,}818^{th}$ Street in the borough of St. Gallen, Switzerland, NY. Your friend Parantap is now at the intersection of $69{,}830^{th}$ Avenue and $90{,}994^{th}$ Street in the borough of Santiniketan, West Bengal, NY. Living costs, of course, have skyrocketed. That's the price for living in Everywhere, New York, NY. Check your inbox. You'll find your new zip code there, along with your adjusted rent.

The 18th Constitutional Crisis

We'd talked so much about the possibility of a constitutional crisis that when the country's 17th constitutional crisis finally arrived, we were relieved. We actually liked it. We grew to understand that it was a great one. It still is. The president declared it the #1 constitutional crisis, the best ever. Coming from the man to whom we already owe sixteen constitutional crises, that's big. Further proof of how ironclad our democracy is, and reason to celebrate. Fourth of July has been moved to July 17th and renamed Constitutional Crisis Day, Memorial and Labor Day Weekends have been packaged as Constitutional Crisis Weekends I & II, and May, September and October, the most beautiful months of the year, have been declared Constitutional Crises Appreciation Months. It's gotten even better since the SEPCC (State of Emergency to Protect the Constitutional Crisis) went into effect. It was then that the president had the genius idea to run for reelection on the platform of a constitutional crisis within the ongoing and likely permanent 17th Constitutional Crisis. He is expected to win by a landslide seventeen weeks before the polls open. It is all we talk about.

The Life Maximizers

They come together to work, live and play. They dine in chef-driven restaurants and shop the world's iconic brands. They receive the most exclusive levels of service, including pet care, plant care and pre-arrival refrigerator stocking. They swim laps while enjoying the unrivaled view of coast and skyline from a 50th floor entirely dedicated to wellness. They curate their own tailored luxury life experience or have it curated from on-site luxury life experience experts. They inspire their young ones with the best interactive experiences for children in sun-filled imagination centers. They cultivate inspired living. They're perfect. They are our future.

My New Neighbors

Jack doesn't live here anymore. John, who now lives here, told me that. It's a corporate decision, he said. John barely knows me but insists on being friends. He even brings an expensive bottle of wine to my place and hugs me. This is too fast for me. Soon, new neighbors arrive, replacing the old. They also want to be friends, bring expensive wine and hugs. I don't know my way around my neighborhood anymore. My new neighbors tell me not to worry. Then I'm replaced. I'm mad at myself I didn't see this coming. I don't like my new neighborhood. I didn't even know it existed. I feel the need to make new friends. I take a bottle of expensive wine, knock on my neighbor's door and hug. I go from door to door, with expensive bottles of wine. It's a corporate decision.

Family Eyes

112 is enough, he said, and died on the day of his 112th birthday. He left behind quite a mess. 112 years of accumulating possessions, renewing stem cells and photo IDs, returning/not returning phone calls, taking leaks and craps is not nothing. Five children, twelve grandchildren, thirty-two great-grandchildren. It gets up there. My favorite of his great-grandchildren is Briony, the granddaughter of his second-born, Caspar. Ellie's daughter. They say she's not Casper's but just look at her eyes. Today, on her great-grandfather's 112th birthday, Briony boards a train. A big party was planned up in Hudson, where he lived. Where he will be buried now. Once Hudson was a run-of-the-mill antique town; now it's a state-of-the-art antique town.

Birthday

I don't know how many people drowned today. Without warning, the Hudson burst its banks and flooded Manhattan. It's Aldana's sixth birthday. Nothing happened to her, mind you; nor to Matt, who seems to be glad that the water ruined his little sister's birthday party; Leonora, my wife, is fine too. We're on the twenty-third floor; the water stopped rising at the twelfth. The Carringtons, our friends on nine, probably didn't make it. For a while, we were all watching the water recede. Matt spotted the first rescue boat, Aldana, her neck bent skyward as usual, saw the first helicopter. The kids are now playing in the living room. Leonora is in the kitchen, preparing sandwiches with whatever will perish first but I keep watching the water.

Patterns

Now don't think the crow flies straight as an arrow, as the adage has it. Not at all. This bird takes half turns, walks in the air, throws partial slips and rolls and even somersaults, and once I've seen one flying overhead with food in its beak. In addition, the crow flight pattern is often complicated by that of the blue jay, peskiest of birds, chasing the crows in pursuit of their food or just for wicked fun. Jays are very intelligent. Okay. You see where this is going. It's a field study. Define the crow flight patterns over a cornfield, a forest, a river, a secret toxic waste site. Present me with a printable 3D model of what New York would look like if it weren't built on a grid but on the way the crows fly.

Pleshcheev

Take Lambert, my downstairs neighbor. She's a barista at Kung Fu Tea and self-identifies as transfeminine neutrois. Chekhov is her choice of favorite writer. That's a great choice but here's the problemo. Chekhov said in that famous letter to Pleshcheev—doesn't matter who that is—that he looks upon labels as prejudiced. Is Chekhov saying Lambert has a prejudice against herself? Is she in need of another favorite writer? Now Facebook has 71 gender labels, but how many favorite writers do you have? Do the math. And we're talking about Chekhov, the most inclusive and humane writer on any favorite-writers list.

Likes

Takashi loves Nigeria, his wife Ibiba's native country, but he hates his work as Press Secretary for the White House. He experiences both feelings with an intensity new to him. I love sex, he says. I am asking you what is it you *like*, Ibiba shoots back. I like the moon, Takashi finally says. I can't say I love it, but I also don't hate it.

Bronx Zoo

You have to attach this to your wheelchair, the woman at the ticket office of the gorilla enclosure says to Corinna, brandishing a tag displaying the wheelchair symbol. Wouldn't people recognize my wheelchair as a wheelchair without a wheelchair symbol attached to it? Corinna points out. While attaching the wheelchair symbol to her wheelchair, the ticket office woman explains that a wheelchair user might get out of their wheelchair unannounced. An empty wheelchair on a path presents a hazard for other visitors. Therefore, a wheelchair must be identified with a tag displaying the wheelchair symbol identifying the wheelchair as a wheelchair at all times. Corinna is considering again pointing out that a wheelchair self-identifies as a wheelchair even without the tag displaying the wheelchair symbol, but she's eager to see the great apes. Upon leaving the gorilla enclosure the tag displaying the wheelchair symbol must be returned to the ticket office, the ticket office woman declares.

Equilibrium

No more news, Eli announced. He removed all the gadgets from his house that were linked to electricity, including the phone, that notorious harbinger of news. Given what a news-junkie-slash-chatterbox she was, he asked Lorrie, his girlfriend of seven years, to move out. He boarded up the windows, stopped emptying his physical mailbox. The local grocery store agreed to regularly deliver whatever they thought he needed. They left the boxes and bags in the backyard, where Eli would pick them up in the middle of the night. On one of those nights, wearing headphones and dark glasses, it occurred to Eli that he hadn't yet taken care of another source of news: his thoughts. Hunkering down in the crawlspace under the staircase he had built for this purpose, he emptied his mind in deep meditation. Soon he was calm again. Briefly, he felt the urge to tell Lorrie about it; but she knew him so well so she'd know somehow. What Eli couldn't know was that Lorrie, out there in the world somewhere, was telling her story about the man who couldn't take the news any longer to anyone would listen.

Again

Felix says he can't consider an experiment this successful a mistake, huge or otherwise. I say that even if the premise was correct, the outcome certainly wasn't. In his superior way, Felix sips his lukewarm water that's supposed to calm his stomach and says he calculated the moment when a city has reached PC (Peak Change) 100% correctly. I have a jovial gulp of my beer and say there can be no doubt that less change is good and that we all need a breather from everything constantly changing faster—but Felix interrupts me to say that his method of inducing HF (Hypergyrochronical Freeze) was beyond scientific doubt—but no more change ever? I finish my sentence. Your HF was so *successful* that now the entire world is in a loop! Felix looks hurt. I'm so close to get him to admit that his experiment was an epic failure. See, successful, a winner, he says, quickly regaining his composure, and I can't help myself to remind him it was a huge mistake.

Crawl

Crawl toward me, Phil shouts in the hallway. Please do not shoot me, Dan pleads, dropping to the floor and starting to crawl toward Phil. If you make a mistake, there is a very real possibility that you will be shot, Phil shouts. The hotel is the La Quinta Inn & Suites, Mesa, AZ. The rifle Phil is pointing at Dan is a semi-automatic Colt AR-15. Dan, 26, is a pest control worker, married, with two daughters. Phil, 25, is a police officer, investigating a report of someone seen pointing a gun out of a fifth-floor window. My grandson Luke, 7, is a second-grader and has a younger sister, Stevie. His right leg is an inch longer than his left leg because of a condition called hemihyperplasia. Please do not shoot me, Dan says again as he reaches to pull up his pants. Phil fires five times. Dan dies on the floor of the hallway of the La Quinta Inn & Suites, Mesa, AZ. Each time Luke watches the video he also says, Please do not shoot me. Today Luke is not wearing his orthopedic shoe that evens out his legs.

Winner

Dad, would I go to prison if Tom got shot by a cop? my son Phil asks. He turns his computer so I can see the screen. Look, he says, agitated, it says here that a cop shot this guy in the back and that his best friend who was with him was sentenced to 32 years in prison. What are you talking about, Phil? I laugh. You will be the cop.

Main Street

Rolling down Main Street, his wheelchair broke down, and now he's in Mattituck, Long Island. It was as though a door opened, and he'd walked through it. But he can't walk. And there isn't a door. A hole opened up and sucked him in. Sinkholes are everywhere now.

Creation Myth

Spirits are roaming the world in search for us. Murdered in our sleep, they have nowhere to return.

Brief History of Mankind

The greatest gardener is god, the gardener said.
Tend to the garden or get out.

The plan is what changes.

Would you please go over to that loud table and ask them to talk about something more interesting?

We're just metaphors for birds.

Have you already been misin-
formed today?

& Look for these Reprobate/GobQ titles:

El Gato Eficaz /Deathcats, Luisa Valenzuela (winner 2019 Carlos Fuentes Prize), tr., Jonathan Tittler (*en-face* bilingual ed.), ISBN: 978-1-93566-234-1 $13

↘↗

A White Concrete Day: Poems, 1978 — 2013, Douglas Spangle (2nd ed.), ISBN:

ISBN 978-1-62847-660-6 $15

↘↗

The Art of Waking Up: 62 Poems & a Song of Despair, Brenda Taulbee, ISBN:

978-1-63068-129-6 $15

↘↗

Breakfast: 43 Poems, Coleman Stevenson, ISBN: 978-1-943844-65-4 $15

↘↗

iM Afraid of aMericans stories, M F McAuliffe, shoegaze books,

ISBN 978-1-94424441-5 $16.00

↘↗

SeaTTle: a novella, M. F. McAULIFFE, shoegaze books, ISBN 978-1-94424441-5, $12.00

↘↗

Appendix A: Sound Seekers: File Under Jazz, Christoph Keller

ISBN 978-1-64764-391-1, $10.00

↘↗

The Jesus He Deserved, & Other Thoughts on War & on Returning, Sean Davis, Matthew Robinson, & Jacob Meeks, ISBN: 978-1-64204-581-9 $17

International trade distrib. through Ingram Spark

↘↗ ↘↗ ↘↗ ↘↗ ↘↗ ↘↗ ↘↗ ↘↗ ↘↗ ↘↗

look for special chappy projects & other textual marvels fr. 2020 & beyond.

Gobshite Quarterly no. 35/36, Winter/Spring 2020, $12

Gobshite Quarterly no. 33/34, Winter /Spring 2019, $12

(avail. online & through var. independent bookstores; issues #19/20 & after distrib. internatinally through Ingram Spark/Lightning Source POD)

A Meaningful Life is a work in progress, a shapeshifting collection of short prose—the kind that dips its cold feet into the warm water of poetry but doesn't dare say *"poem"*—and found photos—the kind that shows you what you don't see even if it is right in front of your eyes. *A Meaningful Life with Bucket I-VII* was first published in 2015 by Lumpish Press in North Carolina (from what I know the press's first and last book), then republished on different paper—newsprint there, natural set 18.3 kgs paper here—by Birutjatio Press in Santiniketan, West Bengal, in English and Bengali, with minor variations and a different set of photographs. *A Meaningful Life 2.0 with Primal Matter I-IX*, also released by Birutjatio in English and Bengali, in 2018, is the project's second incarnation. The eight images (the ninth is the cover image) are, at least in the context of that edition, the binaries of primal matter—heaven/hell, moon/sun, female/male, body/spirit, day/night, order/chaos, mind/matter, good/evil, etc.—of the texts that follow them. The photographs are *"as seen,"* unmanipulated except for some arbitrary distortion of the colors. *America the Beautiful: A Meaningful Life 3.0, Text-Only Edition*, a *Reprobate/GobQ Book*, released and distributed by *GobQ LLC/Gobshite Quarterly*, forgoes pictures entirely in favor of text alone. It's the size of a pocket, not what's generally now called a pocketbook, so it really fits into a pocket and has the potential of becoming a steady companion. *The Practitioner of Physics: A Meaningful Life 4.0, Photo Edition*, to be published by Galerie & Edition Stephan Witschi in Zurich, Switzerland, is now in the early stages of planning. There, the focus will be on the photographs. Texts—in German, translated by Swiss poets Florian Vetsch and Clemens Umbricht—will enter into a more direct, more intense dialogue with the photographs. Texts in different contexts are different texts. — *C.K.*

Christoph Keller (1963), born in St. Gallen, Switzerland, and writing in German and English, is the author of numerous prizewinning novels, plays and essays in German, including *I'd Like My Country Flat* (*Ich hätte das Land gern flach*, 1996), the best-selling memoir *The Best Dancer* (*Der Beste Tänzer*, 2003) about his life with the progressive neuromuscular disease Spinal Muscular Atrophy, *A Worrisome State of Bliss* (stories written in English, 2016) and *The Ground Beneath the Feet* (*Der Boden unter den Füssen*, 2019). In 2017, Alice James Books published *We're On: A June Jordan Reader*, co-edited with Jan Heller Levi. Keller lived in New York for twenty years. In 2018 he heeded the president's advice and went back to where he came from.

www.christophkeller.us

www.ingramcontent.com/pod-product-compliance
Lightning Source LLC
LaVergne TN
LVHW011848060526
838200LV00054B/4239